Daniela Drescher

In the Land of Elves

Floris Books

S0-BCN-901

Deep beneath the woodland ground,
Gemstones sparkle all around.
Brightening the crystal dome
Here the Elf Queen has her home.

When the springtime's sunny rays
First appear with length'ning days
The elves look out without a sound —
You'll catch a glimpse if you're around.

Now the sun comes out to shine,
Wak'ning banks of celandine
The elves are busy, high and low,
Where all the golden petals glow.

Then as dark begins to fall
For hours and hours the crickets call
And elves gaze in the pale moonlight
And watch the starry sky at night.

Each flower and bloom delights the elves,
Their colours bright like they themselves
Each butterfly takes to the air
Lifted by their gentle care.

The days grow cold and leaves turn red,
And elves get up from mossy bed.
Beneath the bushes creeps a mouse
While snails curl snugly in their house.

When autumn comes with mist and shade
The elves go through the leafy glade
Gath'ring nuts of every kind
And all the berries they can find.

Winter's here, the snow is deep
And shiv'ring birds on branches sleep,
The elves come scattering their feed,
Tasty nuts and corn and seed.

Deep beneath the forest floor
The elves are sheltering once more,
The earth goes back to sleep again,
Dreaming of warmth and sun-filled rain.

First published in German in 2005 under the title
Komm mit ins Reich der Zwerge
by Verlag Urachhaus
First published in English in 2005 by Floris Books
Second printing in 2006

© 2005 Verlag Freies Geistesleben & Urachhaus GmbH, Stuttgart
English version © 2005 Floris Books
15 Harrison Gardens, Edinburgh

British Library CIP Data available
ISBN-10: 0-86315-484-0
ISBN-13: 978-086315-484-3
Printed in Denmark